# Nia

## and the

# Polka Dot Blanket

# Project

## The Learning Edition

Written by:

## J. Lavone Roberson

## Illustrated by: Senetha Fuller

To purchase or donate Nia's blanket, please visit www.NowIAmNia.org and click the link for The Polka Dot Blanket Project.

More information about **The Polka Dot Blanket Project** is in the back of the book.

Author Visits

Public Service Projects

Read Alouds

Class Sets and Wholesale Books

Gift Sets & Book Boxes

Follow us on Social Media

## Contact Information

- NowIAmNia@gmail.com
- www.NowIAmNia.org
- @NowIAmNia
- @NowIAmNiaBooks
- @Red_Panda_Artz
- 207-613-6887

Publishing Consulting

Send Us Photos of you reading for a chance to win prizes.

## Copyright Info

Library of Congress Cataloging-in-publication Data
Paperback ISBN (978-1-7365371-3-8:
The text and illustrations were created using Procreate.
Printed in USA.
10 9 8 7 6 5 4 3 2 1
First Edition
February 2021

The Author & Illustrator of "Nia Means Purpose"

**Edits & Reviews:**
Patrice Fortt, BSW
Nehemie Moïse, LMSW
Jackie Roberson, MSW
Jasmin Roberson, BS
Scott Santaniello, Esq.
**Design Consultant:**
Gilbert Mitchell, MBA
Braylynn Smith,

# Dedication

To God. Hallelujah.

To my beloved **Gompa**.
I dedicate this book to you because like
my blanket, you have covered me.
Thank you for teaching me kindness.
You have given our family so much joy
and love. Most importantly, you taught
us to know God, and to love him with all
of our hearts. Thank you. I hope I've
made you happy and proud.
~ (Your 1st Granddaughter) Lavone

To anyone struggling with
anything. We pray you find
a person, place, or thing
that makes you happy.

~Lavone & Senetha

To the little guy who
taught me the meaning
of bravery. My Sun. My
Moon. My Star, and my
Galaxy. My son, Courage
Sabir.
~ Your Mom (Senetha)

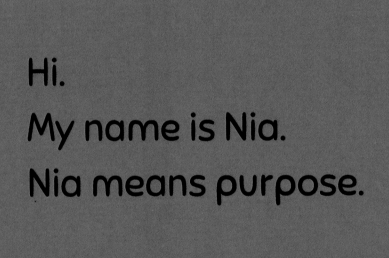

Hi.
My name is Nia.
Nia means purpose.

I always have my blanket
that has so many colors.
I take it everywhere I go;
there's always so much to discover!

I took it out one day at school,
and then I heard the giggles.
"Carrying a blankie is only for babies
to drool on when they're little."

That day I felt embarrassed by it,
the teasing made me sad.
"Those kids are mean –
I love my blanket!"
I had to tell my Dad.

Dad said, "teach them Nia, help them learn why this blanket is so awesome."
When I went to bed that night a new idea did blossom.

For show and tell I told my class why I love my blankie.
I told them stories about the times it helped when I was cranky.

I said...
"My blanket and I are inseparable,
I have it everyday.
It is with me when I am taking a nap,
and when it's time to pray."

"My blanket is so soft and warm.
It's always been by my side.

I hold it close when I am reading,
or when I want to hide."

"My blanket is with me whenever I'm asleep. It's with me when I'm awake.

It's with me when I'm playing with friends, and if I have a belly ache."

People have tried to replace my blanket – but nothing can ever top it.

This thing has **never** left my side,
ever since I got it.

"My blanket helps me most of all
when I feel alone.

Each dot, each color –
reminds me that I'm never on my own."

For some it is a person,
and for others –
it's a place.

"Everyone should have a "thing" that always makes them happy.

Something that helps to change your mood on those days when you're feeling crappy."

I felt so very brave in class, sharing with my peers.
I smiled so big when I finished, and heard all the cheers.

"I have a "thing" too,' Mea said,
She grabbed a scarf out of her backpack,
and put it on her head.

"My *thing* is my doll, I hold it all the time."

"This is my *thing*," Scotty said, holding his
lucky dime.

We all learned a lesson that day,
I had such a great idea.
The first one I told was my Daddy,
I couldn't wait to share.

"I think I know what I will do to try to stop
the teasing..."

He listened and smiled,
I could tell he was proud.
This idea was very pleasing.

"Give people blankets, I love this idea! Sharing is very kind."

We got right to work, the very next day on our blanket design.

"My blanket has been perfect for me,
others should feel the same.
We will call them 'Nia Blankets,'
it'll be my claim to fame!"

My parents were so proud of me.
They thought my idea was perfect.

"We are so proud,
our little Nia, is doing community service.
We always hoped that one day
you'd understand your purpose."

We searched and worked to find blankets,
and different ways to collect.

"Hey Nia,
what do you want to call this plan?"
"The Polka Dot Blanket Project!"

MISSION: Serving communities with new inspirational and amazing opportunities to discern purpose.

The Now I Am Nia Foundation, Inc.

Nia means purpose.

THE PURPOSE PROJECT

The Polka Dot Blanket Project

Nia Selah

A letter from the CEO/Founder of
The Now I Am Nia Foundation, Inc.

about

## The Polka Dot Blanket Project

I founded The Now I Am Nia Foundation, Inc in 2019. The Polka Dot Blanket project was my first organized charity.

I chose to donate blankets because of my love for my own polka dot blanket.

I got my blanket in college, and we were immediately inseparable. It was my first time living away from home, and I needed something cozy. Its bright colors made me happy.

People would always comment on it because it went wherever I went. I have traveled the world with it. It has been with me anytime I've needed it. It comforted me as I went through multiple surgeries, and chemotherapy treatments as well.

One day at the hospital I heard someone ask for a blanket, and I came up with the idea that I should pass out blankets to hospitalized children. I figured a bright and cozy blanket could make them smile. This plan of sharing blankets has now expanded to anyone in need; caregivers, patients, homeless shelters, essential workers, random acts of kindness gifts, etc.

My hope is that the blankets makes people feel "covered" in prayer and love. I want to share the comfort and love my blanket has given me.

So far, The Now I Am Nia Foundation, Inc has donated over 100 blankets since its launch in 2019. To donate toward this charity please visit www.NowIAmNia.org/polkadotblanketproject.

With Love,

# THE PURPOSE PROJECT

## To promote kindness and community.

*"Life's most persistent and urgent question is: What are you doing for others?"*
*- Dr. Martin Luther King Jr.*

### Family:

- Read books as a family, and discuss them.
- Cook as a family and try new recipes.
- Watch documentaries about other cultures.
- Help your family organize your space.
- Choose gently used items in the home to donate.

### Neighborhood:

- Clean up garbage as you see it; don't litter in your neighborhood.
- Offer to take out the trash, shovel, or garden at your neighbors home.
- Create community programs that promote sharing family traditions.
  - Pot Lucks; Cultural celebrations
- Celebrate each other's history and experiences.
  - Black History, Hispanic Heritage, Pride Week
- Create a neighborhood tradition of volunteering with local organizations i.e. homeless shelter, food pantry, community centers, etc.

### Community:

- Find a local charity that supports a topic you are passionate about, and participate in its programming. www.NowIAmNia.org
- Donate cleaning supplies, sanitizer, and masks to shelters.
- Make friends with kids in other schools and communities, and become pen-pals.
- Write funny cards to people in senior care homes or hospitals.
- Draw pictures and/or make *Get Well* cards for people in the hospital.

### Animals:

- Offer to walk an elderly person's pet.
- Donate towels, food, and cleaning supplies to your local animal shelter.

# Transitional Items

*I am with you always, even to the end of the age. Matthew 28:20*

A transitional item, also known as a security blanket, is a comfort item used to provide emotional support in varied situations. Popular transition items are blankets, as seen in this text, and with Linus in the *Charlie Brown* series. Other items are pacifiers, "lucky" socks, heirlooms, or stuffed toys. Whatever item has sentimental meaning, and helps you adjust to changes is a transitional item.

## Nia was teased because of her blanket, but she decided to share blankets with others instead of being embarrassed by hers.

Have you, or someone you know, ever had a transitional item?

_____

What is it?

_____

Where is it?

_____

What made it so special?

_____

_____

_____

_____

Draw a picture of it.

# Social Emotional Learning

Nia chooses to teach her classmates about why she loves her blanket when they tease her. Her choice to teach instead of: avoid school, throw her blanket away, or fight, is an indication of her understanding of some core social emotional strategies.

**Social Emotional Learning** is an essential part of human development. How we interact with people, control our behaviors, and recognize our emotions impacts all of our relationships.

These 5 lessons will help you, or whomever you share this book with, understand the 5 core competencies of social emotional learning.

Essential Questions can be reworded for all ages.

Learning Topics Covered:

- Self Awareness
- Self Control
- Diversity
- Equity
- Inclusion
- Peer Relationships
- Conflict Resolutions
- Goal Setting
- Growth Mindset
- and more...

# 1. Self Awareness:

## Understanding how your thoughts and/or emotions impact your behavior.

### Activities:
-Journaling
-Prayer/Meditation
-Reading
-Decorating your own space.
-Planning your day (scheduling).
-Choosing activities with family.
-Crafting.
-Write down positive affirmations to yourself.

### Standards:
• Describe and/or recognize emotions an[d] how they can affect an individual's behavio[r]
• Identify values, attitudes and beliefs.
• Demonstrate ways to make and keep friends and/or meaningful relationships.

## Essential Questions:

• How do I recognize my feelings?
• Do I know how to name those feelings?
• How do my feelings impact my actions and thoughts?
• What makes me unique and special?
• What helps me feel joy, and happiness?
• What positive words would I use to describe myself? What positive words would my friends use to describe me?

# 2. Self-Management. Being able to regulate your behaviors in different situations to help you achieve your goals.

## Standards:

- Demonstrate cooperative behavior in a group.
- Understand the need for self-control and/or emotional regulation, and how to practice it.

**Activities:**

- Journaling
- Listening to calming music.
- Prayers/Meditation
- Talk to someone you trust.
- Exercise.
- Share your thoughts with peers.

## Essential Questions:

- How can I help my peers be productive?
- What strategies can I use to help me in this moment?
- What is bothering me, and who can support me to with it?
- How can I express how I am feeling?
- How have my peers influenced my thinking and actions?
- What can I do today to help someone else?

# 3. Social Awareness

## Empathy, respect, and appreciation for others.

DIVERSITY
EQUITY
INCLUSION

### Standards:

- Demonstrate ways to communicate care, empathy, respect and responsibility for others without bias, abuse, discrimination or harassment based on, but not limited to, race, color, sex, religion, national origin, sexual orientation, ancestry, marital status, mental retardation, mental disorder and learning and/or physical disability.

### Essential Questions:

- Why is it important to understand cultural differences?
- If I notice someone being mistreated because of their differences what action can I take?
- What are ways to celebrate, and learn about the differences that are around me?
- How do my beliefs, values, and cultural background influence my actions?

# 4. Relationship Skills

## Listening and responding to maintain healthy relationships with others.

**Activities:**

-Book clubs
- Video chatting
- Taking walks as a group.
- Playing/Creating games together.
- Telling stories.
- Listening to new information.
- Shaw & Tell or Share Time
- Pen Pals
-Drawing pictures together.

### Standards:

- Demonstrate initiative in using appropriate skills for resolving conflicts peacefully and encouraging others to do the same.
- Demonstrate an understanding of the components of communication skills, attending, listening, responding

### Essential Questions:

- How do we continue to work together even when we disagree?
- Based on what you read, what are some ways that Nia's friends showed that they respected her?
- What words best describe Nia?
- What qualities make you a good friend?

# 5. Decision Making: Using evidence, research, and facts to make positive choices.

## Standards:

- Describe the influence of peer pressure on the choices you make.
- Apply effective problem solving and decision making skills to make safe and healthy choices.

**Activities:**
- Breath
- Read non-fiction books.
- (Scenario Games) Reflect on things that have happened to others and write/discuss what you would do if it happened to you.
- Brainstorm your ideas before making a decision.
- Make an action plan
- Perform skits with family/friends.
- Do scavenger hunts
- Complete puzzles

## Essential Questions:

- How does peer pressure impact my decisions?
- What is the impact of teasing someone?
- If someone hurts my feelings how can I handle it in a positive way?
- What are the consequences and benefits of a decision without thought?
- How can I make it right with someone I may have hurt?

Goggins II, L. (2017) The Emergence of Social Emotional Learning and the Implications for the Black child. *Black Child Journal:Education and the Black Child* , Summer, 51 - 63.

# Jacquelyn "Lavone" Roberson

Author

is from Norwalk, CT. She is an educator and two time cancer survivor. She writes about Nia, a fictional character who helps people learn purpose. Lavone is The CEO and Founder of The Now I Am Nia Foundation, Inc, where she serves communities in need through various philanthropic projects. Lavone is an alumni of Hampton University and a member of Delta Sigma Theta Sorority, Incorporated. As a teacher she was selected to be in the Nation's First Quad-D Lab Classroom cohort. When she is not writing, teaching, or working in the community she enjoys traveling and spending time with her god children. To learn more, donate, or book for speaking engagements please visit www.NowIAmNia.org and follow us @NowIAmNiaBOOKS. 1 Corinthians 10:31

## Illustrator

Senetha Fuller resides in Philadelphia, PA. She specializes in "urban art" but can create custom art using different mediums. It has always been her passion to inspire through her art @Red_Panda_Artz

Made in the USA
Middletown, DE
28 March 2022

63287273R00024